Monday Popular Concerts.

Director—Mr. S. ARTHUR CHAPPELL.

Five Hundred and Second Concert.*

PROGRAMME FROM THE WORKS OF

Various Masters.

MONDAY EVENING, JANUARY 25th, 1875.

Part I.

QUARTET, in G major, Op. 54, No. 2, for two Violins,
Viola, and Violoncello.   *Haydn.*

(Second performance at the Popular Concerts.)

Allegro con brio—G major.
Allegretto—C major.
Minuetto and Trio—G major.
Presto (Finale)—G major.

Madame NORMAN-NERUDA,

Herr L. RIES, Herr STRAUS, and Signor PIATTI.

Nothing more purely and legitimately Haydn than this
quartet exists in its composer's almost inexhaustible repertory.

---

* Seventeenth Concert of the Seventeenth Season.

The *allegro con brio* sets out with the following spirited and well-developed theme :—

The foregoing is cited at unusual length, because, with the exception of an occasional episode, as attentive hearers will not fail to observe, it forms the *substratum* of the entire movement. Here, for example, is an episode in question :—

This half close brings back the leading theme in the original key; but, as will be seen below, it soon gives way to a counter theme, in the orthodox dominant :—

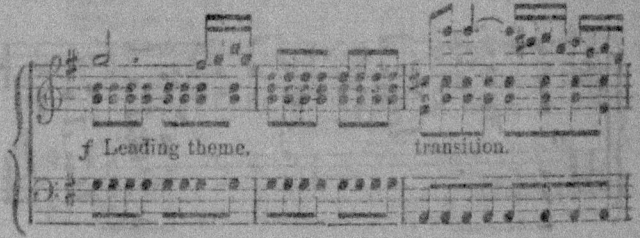

The further development of this second subject is made noticeable by the introduction of a prominent feature in the leading theme (𝄢) :—

After a full close in D, comes the peroration, in which, as will be observed, the same phrase (𝄢) again plays a conspicuous part :—

The foregoing materials are all made use of in the second division of the *allegro*, which, like the first, is meant to be repeated. The elaborate development of this "free *fantasia*" must, however, speak for itself. The movement comes to an end with a reference to the leading theme, beginning on an interrupted cadence (*), and twice more invaded by the particular phrase which has already been thrice referred to ( ):—

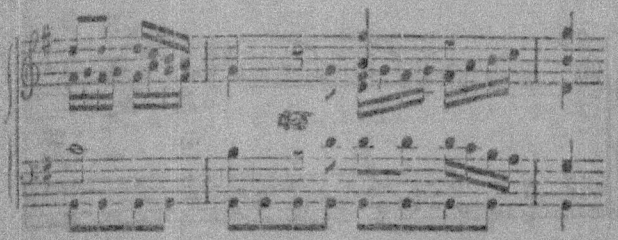

Haydn himself has written no more homogeneous movement than this *allegro con brio*.

Allegretto (theme).

Further quotation from so unpretending and simply constructed a movement would be superfluous.

Minuetto.

Trio.

1st Violin *tacet.*

Presto (leading theme).

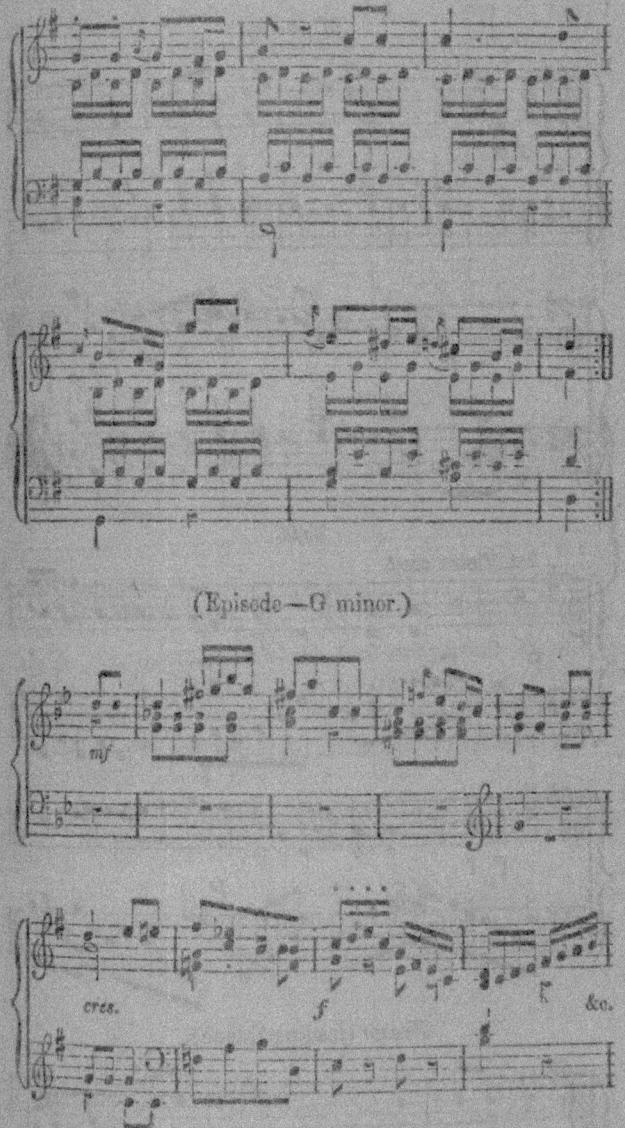

(Episode—G minor.)

This movement is in the *rondo* form. The theme re-
appears several times, and each time in a modified shape as
regards all except the melody, short episodes always pre-

5 A

824

paring the *rentrée*. A brilliant *coda*, for the four instruments in unison, introduces us to a last glimpse of the theme, on a dominant pedal :—

One of the gayest and freshest of its nearly always cheerful composer's movements of the kind, and sparkling with quiet humour, it can never fail to impress and charm.

The Quartet in G major was first introduced by M. Sainton, Herr L. Ries, Mr. Zerbini, and Signor Piatti, at the second concert of the seventeenth season—November 14, 1874.

LIEDER, Miss ANTOINETTE STERLING. *Rubinstein.*

"WALDEINSAMKEIT."

Waldeinsamkeit, du grünes Revier,
Wie liegt so weit die Welt von hier,
Schlaf nur, wie bald kommt der Abend schön,
Durch den stillen Wald die Quellen geh'n.

Die Mutter Gottes wacht,
Mit ihrem Sternenkleid
Bedeckt sie dich sacht
In der Waldeinsamkeit.
Gute Nacht, gute Nacht!

DIE WALDHEXE.

Vorbei, vorbei, durch Feld und Wald,
Zu Ross in wilder Eile,
Was willst du schwebende Gestalt
Mit deinem Wink zur Weile?

Mein Bett ist nicht auf grüner Haid,
Und nicht im schatt'gen Walde,
Es wartet mein die schönste Maid,
Und Liebe ruft: "komm balde!"

Lass ab, lass ab, begleitend Weib,
Dein Arm ist viel zu luftig,
Dein Blick zu todt, dein schlanker Leib
Zu kalt und nebelduftig.

Mein Lieb hat weiss'ren Arm als du,
Hat Augen wie zwei Sterne,
Und küsst, und herzt, und lacht dazu.
Was drohst du mir von ferne?

Der Reiher kreischt, es schlägt das Ross,
Die blutgespornten Flanken,
Das Weib wird dreist und riesengross,
Und wilder die Gedanken.

Vorbei, vorbei, wie Fittig rauscht,
Es nickt herab vom Baume,
Es huscht und hascht, es lugt und lauscht,
Schon greift sie nach dem Zaume.

Jetzt hat sie seinen Arm gefasst,
Umher beginnt's zu dunkeln,
Es schwillt herauf, es drückst die Last,
Des Weibes Augen funkeln.

Zwei Sprünge vom gestürzten Thier,
Da liegt in dunkeln Walde
Der Reiter todt im Arme ihr,
Und Liebe ruft: "komm balde!"

SONATA, in D major, Op. 10, No. 3, for
Pianoforte alone.*   *Beethoven.*

(Thirteenth performance at the Popular Concerts.)

Presto—D major.
Largo e mesto—D minor.
Minuetto, Allegro—D major:
with Trio—G major.
Rondo, Allegro—D major.

Madlle. MARIE KREBS.

In this very fine work, the most vigorous, if not the most
absolutely beautiful† of the sonatas belonging to the period of
which it may be said to form the climax, Beethoven, entirely
ignoring all previous models, even of his own creation, gives
the rein to his Pegasus, and soars far beyond the reach of
ordinary thinkers. Happily it is one of the best known of the
wonderful sonata-family that sprang from the imaginative
brain of the composer, and therefore does not require so close
an analysis as several of the early series to which it belongs,
and of which it is the crowning glory. The impetuous unison
with which the *presto* opens :—

—the question, as it were, to which the harmonious phrase
that follows, after the pause, is a reply :—

—will be recognized at once by all who have attempted, or
heard others attempt to play the sonata. Nor less readily
the continuation of the first subject, in a new form (the unison
abandoned), which breaks off upon another pause, now on the

* No. 7 of Beethoven's Sonatas, edited by Mr. CHARLES HALLÉ
—published by Chappell and Co 50, New Bond Street.
† the E flat Sonata, Op. 7, is on the whole most fairly entitled
to that distinction.

ominant of the relative minor—a second question, to which the subjoined quaint subject is a second answer :—

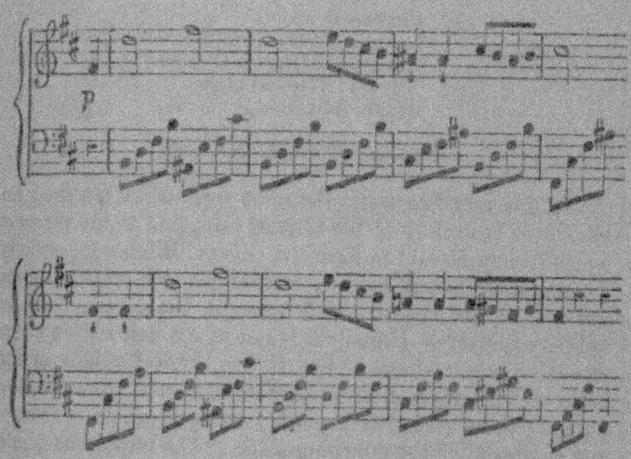

The spirited working up of this, until we arrive at the counter-subject, in the orthodox dominant :—

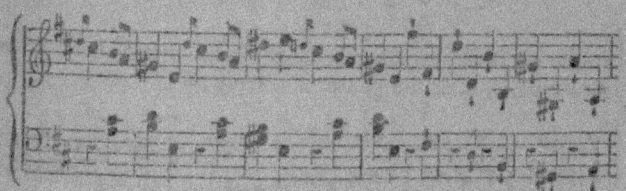

—the series of progressions which, built upon the continuation of the second subject :—

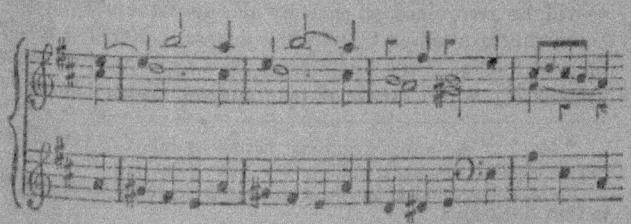

—transport us into other regions of tone, until we are unexpectedly forced back again :——

—the playful counter-theme that ensues, now given to the right hand, now to the left :——

—and the last new phrase :——

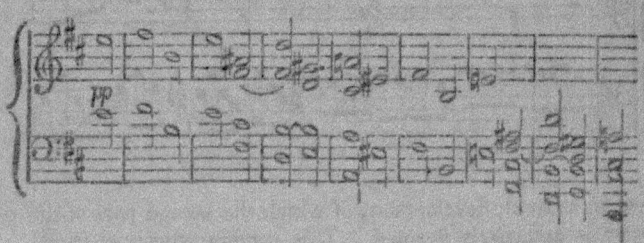

—which brings us to the *coda*, or termination of the first part, are, one and all, calculated to stamp themselves indelibly on the memory. A first part wealthier in ideas is hardly to be found even among Beethoven's pianoforte sonatas: but, as if not half exhausted, the invention of the great composer still further disports itself in the second, which, after the leading theme has been given out in the tonic minor—another pause, as it were, in anticipation of another query—starts off suddenly with a wholly fresh answer, in an unanticipated key, and on a tonic bass :—

The foregoing is merely the preamble to an episode, commencing thus :—

—to an elaborate development of which the second part of the *presto* is exclusively devoted. This confers unwonted freshness on the recapitulation of the first, with which, allowing for the accustomed transpositions of subordinate themes (from B

minor to E minor, and from A major to D major), it is iden-
tical as far as the *coda*.   In this *coda* :—

—one of Beethoven's most fanciful—the composer again
exerts his ingenuity on a phrase in the continuation of the
second subject, which forms the basis of the striking progres-
sion cited in the previous page but one ; and the *presto* termi-
nates with an animated *crescendo*.

The *largo* (in D minor) is the second of those slow movements which not only raise the pianoforte to the dignity of an
orchestra, but attain the highest dramatic expression.   The
slow movements of the Quartet in F, Op. 18, and the Trio in
D, Op. 70, (No. 2), both of which are in D minor, alone surpass it (if indeed they may be fairly said to surpass it) in
depth of sentiment.   The leading theme will be recognized
by a few bars :—

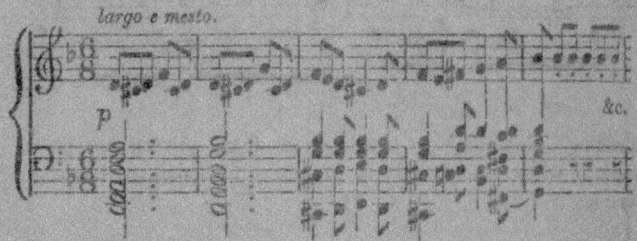

Equally so the counter-theme which grows out of it :—

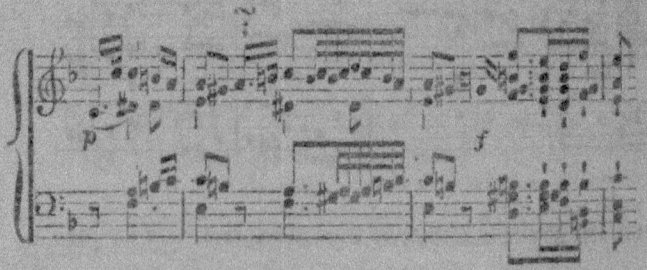

Not less familiar is the lovely episode, which a fragment may recall :—

—and which affords a transient gleam of consolation amid the dark gloom that everywhere else pervades the *largo*. The impassioned *crescendo*—built upon the leading theme, and commencing as subjoined :—

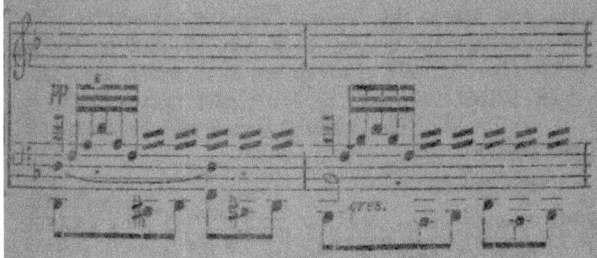

—subsiding gradually, at the climax from *fortissimo* to *pianissimo*, when the melody is broken into disjointed fragments :—

—as if the grief the composer tried to express were too profound for utterance; and the unspeakable sadness of the concluding bars :—

—are among the highest inspirations of Beethoven, who seldom more emphatically vindicated his right to the denomination of "tone-poet" than in this grand and impressive slow movement.

The *minuetto*, with its tuneful theme :—

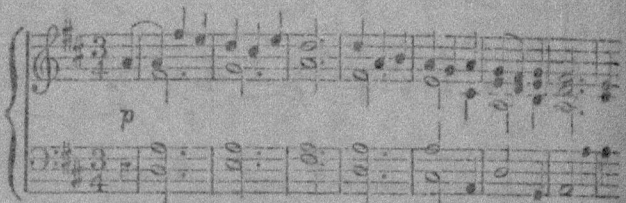

—comes after the *largo* like the innocent smile of a maiden; the simpler melody of the *trio*—with its accompaniment of triplets :—

—like the unconscious prattling of a child. The quartet in D major (Op. 18) has a *minuetto* in the same key, which, for cheerful and melodious beauty, may be compared with this.

The *rondo* is one of Beethoven's most sparkling, original, and *ad captandum* movements. It seems a sort of distant prophecy of the *finale* to the Trio in D (Op. 70), to which—in its frequent pauses and playfully capricious character—it bears a family resemblance. The opening theme affords a fair indication of what is to ensue :—

The second section of this leading subject proclaims no less clearly that melody is about to play its part :—

The second theme, which would settle in A, if it could—only that Beethoven will not allow it emphatically to declare itself—is quite in keeping with the fanciful structure of the rest :—

These are the chief elements out of which the *rondo* is built. In the *presto* (first movement) it will be rememebred, the second part contains a sudden transition into B flat. A similar transition occurs in the *rondo*—but at the end of the first part, instead of at the beginning of the second. The episode, to which this transition leads, sets out as follows :—

There is no other episode, from this point to the end of the *rondo*. The first and second sections of the principal theme form the subject matter; and their treatment is as ingenious as it is fanciful. In none of his last movements is Beethoven more thoroughly original; in none does he play with his theme more felicitously, or present and represent it under more unexpected aspects.

The original title-page of the three sonatas, Op. 10, is as follows:—" *Trois sonates pour le Clavecin ou Piano-Forte, Composées et Dediées à Madame la Comtesse de Browne, née de Vietinghoff, par Louis van Beethoven. Œuvre* 10, *à Vienne, chez Joseph Eder, sur le Graben.*" They were published by subscription, and advertised as having appeared on the 26th of September, 1798.

The Sonata in D major was first introduced by Mr. Charles Hallé, at the 20th concert of the second season— April 30, 1860.

END OF THE FIRST PART.

*** Madlle. MARIE KREBS will perform on one of Messrs. JOHN BROADWOOD and SONS' Concert Grand Pianofortes.

Entr' Acte.

BEETHOVEN IN HIS LETTERS.

The world's heroes are too often seen only in the fashion of the distinguished lords and gentlemen, whose portraits in oil, life-size, adorn the walls of our public buildings. That is to say, we view them *en grande tenue*, posed for effect, and with a back-ground which, as a rule, is a purely fancy sketch. As far as Beethoven is concerned this need not be. We can know him, if we will, as other than the wild-haired, scowling man, whom engravings represent jotting down mighty thoughts, with his back to a thunder-cloud. The particulars of his life, his sayings and doings, have been recorded by zealous pens, and these are at our service; best of all, his letters have been collected, and by them the man is shown in his own light, not possibly distorted by the false colouring of others. We would commend a study of Beethoven's letters to all who have received without question the common idea of his character. The illustrious composer is thought of, for the most part, as a rough, morose, cynical, and unlovely man, one whom genius alone made endurable. That there is no foundation for this we do not say, because heavy trials produced their inevitable result upon a proud and sensitive nature. We do aver, however, that the real character of the man was something very different, and need only the support of his letters to establish the case. A few examples of the testimony borne by these witnesses who cannot lie, will assuredly be interesting, and, to make their evidence more conclusive, we will cull only from the epistles of his later years, when the iron of a miserable life had entered deeply into his soul.

We have Beethoven's own assurance that he was adapted by nature to enjoy the pleasures of social intercourse, and piteous were his complaints of the isolation to which deafness condemned him. The geniality that would have made him a favourite every-where breaks out now and then in the letters to his intimate friends. Writing to Bolderini, he winds up with "Farewell, Knight Falstaff; do not be too dissipated; read the gospel and be converted." Haslinger gets from him this piece of advice: "Sing daily the epistles of St. Paul, and daily visit Father Werner, who can show you in his little book how to go straight to heaven. See how anxious I am about the welfare of your soul." To Schindler he says with quiet humour: "The tailor comes to-day, still (Poor Beethoven was short of money) I hope to be able to get rid of him for the present by a few polite phrases." Schindler, by the way, was the favourite target at which Beethoven aimed his good-tempered jokes. At one time the composer's future bio-grapher is a "Samothracian vagabond," at another "Most worthy ragamuffin of Epirus and Brundusium," at another, "Master flash in the pan, and wide of the mark! full of reasons, yet devoid of reason," at another "Il Sinnore nobile, Papageno Schindler,"

and at another simply " Wiseacre." Once the master wrote to
Grillparzer about his friend, "That obtrusive appendage, Schindler, has long been most obnoxious to me." Over and over again
does this pleasant banter appear, spite of the great troubles and
small worries that made Beethoven their prey; and it is not
difficult to see how such passages reveal the true nature of the
man. If we did not know the perfect devotion he entertained for
art, his affliction might seem a providential interference on behalf
of art. Even as it is, we know not how much the world has
gained by the barrier which kept Beethoven out of the society he
was no less fitted to adorn than to enjoy.

As regards the capacity for loving with which Beethoven was
endowed, his letters show it to have been of no ordinary kind.
How he cherished an affection for the Countess Guicciardi—how,
in fact, his ardent nature was always seeking fellowship with
some congenial spirit—is well known. He addresses the Countess
as " My Angel! my all! my second self!" and says "Love demands all, and has a right to do so; and thus it is that I feel
towards you and you towards me. * * * * My heart
is overflowing with all I have to say to you. Ah! there are
moments when I find that speech is actually nothing. Continue
to be ever my true and only love, my all: as I am yours!" To
Bettina von Arnim he writes:—"The most beautiful themes
stole from your eyes into my heart, which shall yet enchant the
world when Beethoven no longer directs. If God vouchsafes to
grant me a few more years of life, I must then see you once more,
my dear, most dear friend, for the voice within, to which I always
listen, demands this. Spirits may love one another, and I shall
ever woo yours. Your approval is dearer to me than all else in
the world." Thus could the rugged misanthrope, as some called
him, pour out the treasures of his heart where he was sure of a
sympathetic response, but we see him do it even more lavishly in
the letters to his ward and nephew, Carl. This young man had
been left in Beethoven's charge while yet a lad, and upon him the
great composer lavished a wealth of affection, which was not only
wasted but abused. Carl was a graceless fellow, and when his
uncle addressed him as " My dear young scamp," Beethoven was
nearer the truth than love permitted him to believe. But the
uncle remained faithful to the nephew through both evil and good
report, bearing patiently with the rejection of his counsels, and
ever receiving the Prodigal (who often returned when reduced
to swine-husks) with open arms. We must give a few examples
of the old "misanthrope's" enduring affection. He writes to Carl,
"You must come to me on Sunday;' but the scapegrace has
more congenial pursuits, and Beethoven meekly replies, "I have
no wish to deprive you of any pleasure, were I only sure that
you would spend your Sunday properly away from me. Reproving
his ward for some disobedience, Beethoven says "If you find the
Pactum oppressive, then in God's name I resign you to His holy
keeping;" following this up, as though alarmed for the result,
with "Do not be afraid to come to me to-morrow." Again he
reproves; "My heart has been so deeply wounded by your
deceitful conduct that it is difficult to forget it;" whereupon Carl
stays away from his uncle's house, and the old man writes, "I
wish you at least to come here on Sundays. In vain do I ask for
an answer. God help you and me. * * * * My con-

tinued solitude only still further enfeebles me, and really my
weakness often amounts to a swoon. Oh! do not further grieve
me." Six days after, Beethoven sends his nephew sixty-two
florins for a new suit, and, [after advice about the cloth, adds:
"Now farewell, my darling! deserve the name; I embrace you,
and hope you will be my good, studious, noble son." In very
warm weather his thoughts go to poor Carl, and so does a letter
beginning—"As in this heat you may, perhaps, wish to bathe, I
send you two more florins." Verily, what an uncle is here! Carl
wants more money, and gets it with this advice: "Now pray
practise economy, for you certainly receive too much cash. I
rejoiced when I could assist my poor parents; what a contrast are
you in your conduct to me. Thriftless boy, farewell!" The heat
continues, and Beethoven sends another florin, with "Do
not neglect your bathing; continue well, and guard against illness.
Spend your money on good objects alone. Be my dear son."
Carl again misbehaves—borrows money of a "mean old kitchen
wench," and is sternly asked "Why such hypocrisy?" Then
comes the salve: "But do not be uneasy; I shall continue to
care for you as much as ever;" upon which Carl went on as
badly as ever. One more quotation must suffice, Beethoven
writes to the ne'er-do-weel: "My dear son, say no more; only
come to my arms; not one harsh word shall you hear. You shall
be received as lovingly as ever, * * * only come. Come to the
faithful heart of your father." We might multiply these proofs
of Beethoven's great loving spirit, but the foregoing will suffice
to show that he was not the savage popularly supposed; that, in
short, his nature was tender and affectionate, though circumstances
overlaid it with an appearance of unloveliness.

JOSEPH BENNETT.

A PIANOFORTE COMBAT.

In the summer of 1846, Liszt and Chopin, those two heroes of
the piano, were enjoying the charming hospitality of Madame
Georges Sand, at her Château of B., near Paris. Concerning the
meeting of the two great artists, the latter of whom already bore
the germs of death in his heart, M. Charles Rollant gives in
the *Temps* an interesting description, from which we extract the
following:—

"One morning in May a select party was assembled in the
large drawing-room of the friendly mansion. Literary and artistic
celebrities from Paris, and gentlemen of the neighbourhood with
their wives—all young and enthusiastic—were gathered around
their clever and graceful hostess. Liszt played a Nocturne of
Chopin's, embellishing it, in his genial manner, with shakes, tre-
molos, arpeggios, &c., not one of which was marked in the original.
For some time Chopin exhibited various marks of disapprobation.
At last he could contain himself no longer. Going up to the piano,
he said, in his well-known phlegmatic tone, to Liszt:—

"'My good friend, may I beg that, when you do me the honour
of playing anything of mine, to play it as it is written, or to play
something else. Only Chopin has the right to alter Chopin.'

"'Then play yourself,' answered Liszt, rising.

"'Very good,' said Chopin. At this moment the lamp was extinguished by a moth, which had flown into the flame. Some one wanted to light the lamp again. 'No,' said Chopin, 'put out the lights; I like the moon.' He then played a whole hour and more. How he played it is useless to attempt describing. There are impressions which may be felt, but cannot possibly be rendered in words. When the magician ended, all eyes were moist with tears. Liszt embraced his friend, and said cordially, 'My dear fellow, you were right. The works of a mind like yours are sacred. It is sacrilege to touch them. You are the true prophet, compared to whom I am only a bungler.'

" 'Not so,' replied Chopin, with animation; 'but each has his own style, that is all. You know that no one on earth can play Weber and Beethoven as you can, and I now ask you to play us the *Adagio* of the C sharp minor ("Moonlight") Sonata, but seriously, and as you can play it if you like.' Liszt played the movement, throwing his whole heart and soul into his task. A completely different kind of emotion was apparent among those present. It is true that they wept, and even sobbed; but it was not the gentle tears which Chopin caused to flow, but the "cruel tears" of which Othello speaks. Under Liszt's hands, the melodies did not glide gently into the heart; they forced their way into it, like a dagger—it was no longer an elegy, but a drama. Chopin, at all events, thought that he had eclipsed Liszt. He even boasted of it, actually saying, 'How angry he was.' Liszt heard of these words, and resolved to revenge himself.

" A few evenings subsequently, the company were again assembled in the same place. Liszt asked Chopin to play, and after various excuses Chopin consented. Liszt now requested that all the lights should be a second time extinguished, and the curtains drawn, so that the darkness might be complete. This having been done, Liszt, hastily whispering a few words to Chopin, who had just sat down at the piano, took Chopin's place. Chopin, who was far from suspecting what his brother-artist intended, threw himself into the nearest arm-chair. Liszt now performed, thanks to his wonderful memory, precisely the same pieces which Chopin had played on the previous evening, imitating, moreover, so marvellously his rival's style and manner, that it was impossible not to be taken in; and everyone was taken in accordingly. There was a repetition of the same spell, and of the same emotion. When the latter had reached its highest pitch, Liszt quickly struck a match, with which he lighted the tapers on the piano. The result was a general exclamation of surprise: 'What! Is it you?'—'As you perceive!'—'Why, we thought it was Chopin!'—'What do you think of that?' enquired Liszt of his rival. 'I say what everyone else says: I also thought it was Chopin!' 'You see,' observed the virtuoso, rising, 'that Liszt can be Chopin if he pleases;' adding with a sarcastic smile, 'but can Chopin be Liszt?'

" This was a public challenge, which, however, Chopin would not, or dared not, accept, and thus was Liszt revenged by Liszt himself."—*Musical World.*

Part II.

TRIO, No. 1, in G minor, Op. 8, for Pianoforte, Violin, and Violoncello. *Chopin.*

(First performance at the Popular Concerts.)

Allegro con fuoco—G minor.
Scherzo—G major; with Trio—C major.
Adagio—E flat major.
Finale, allegretto—G minor.

Mme. MARIE KREBS, Mme. NORMAN-NÉRUDA, and Signor PIATTI.

This work, belonging to Chopin's early time, exhibits few of those characteristic features that distinguished his ripe maturity. Its wholly independent form, however, in the opening *allegro*, points to the man who, years later, became a master possessed with a striking individuality which none could fairly question. The briefest possible references to the prominent themes in each movement of the trio will suffice :—

Allegro con fuoco (preamble).

(Leading theme.)

(Tributary.)

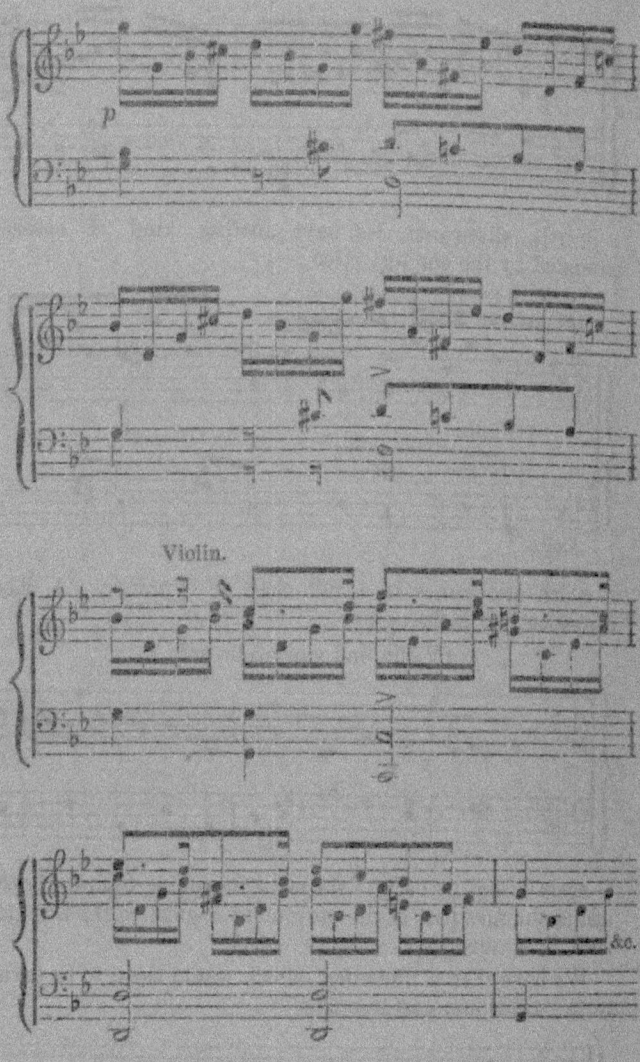

Violin.

"Our analysts" will not fail to observe that up to this point we are in the key of G minor. Further on, a half close on the dominant brings us to an episode, which is also in G minor :—

(Episode—violin and violoncello only.)

Shortly afterwards, we have another kind of episode, generated by the one just cited :—

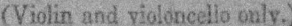

—which also comes to a full close in G minor. A short digression into E flat :—

(Violin and violoncello only.)

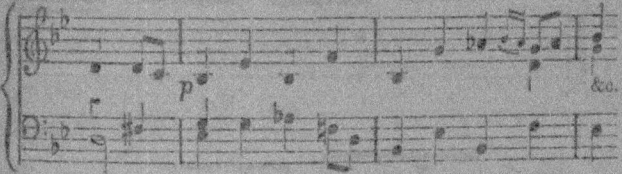

—again brings us back to the same inevitable *Stand-Punkt*; and as the first part of the movement begins, so the first part ends, in G minor.

We have then a transition, which would seem to be taking us to " fields and pastures new" :—

—but no; this is only to lead back again to G minor, for a repetition of the first part :—

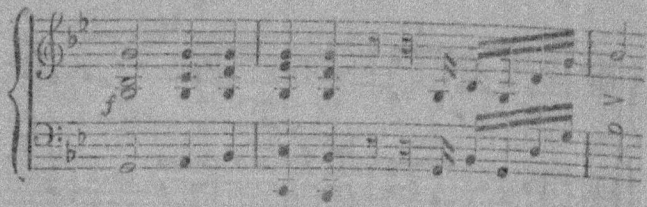

The conception of this first part is quite peculiar to Chopin. Of the second part, or free *fantasia*, which, through another transition, brings us to D minor :—

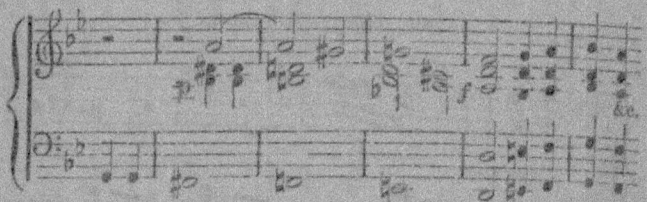

—it is unnecessary to give any detailed analysis. The return to the leading theme, with its preamble, comes in due course; the other themes reappear with modifications that must speak for themselves; and the movement ends with a brief reference to the opening preamble, more than once cited.

Scherzo.

Trio (C major).

Adagio.

Finale, Allegretto (theme.)

Chopin produced in all, about seventy works—including two grand concertos for piano with orchestral accompaniments, two grand sonatas for piano solo, a sonata for pianoforte and violoncello, other pieces with orchestral accompaniments, several books of studies and preludes, together with a large number of *nocturnes, polonaises, ballades,* scherzos, mazurkas, variations, &c. These do not include his posthumous works, two volumes of which have appeared—the last consisting of *sixteen Polish songs,* numbered Op. 47 (why it is difficult to say, "Op. 47" being affixed to his *Troisième Ballade,* in A flat), and published some years ago, with the original Polish words, and German versions by Herr Gumbert, the popular lyric poet. That Chopin, however, excelled less in works of "*longue haleine*" than in those of smaller pretensions, will hardly be denied. His *Etudes*, his *Preludes*, his *Valses*, his *Nocturnes*, and, above all, his Mazurkas, are quite enough to save him from oblivion, whatever may eventually become of his concertos and sonatas. The varied manner in which he has said the same thing some fifty times over will go further than anything else to prove that Chopin's talent, whatever its eccentricities and failings, was decidedly inventive. The best of the Mazurkas are, without question, those that smell least strongly of the lamp; those which, harmonised in the least affected manner, are easiest to play, and bear the closest affinity to (in some cases are almost echoes of) the national dance tunes of his country. Many of them are gems, as faultless as they are attractive, from whatever point of view regarded; others, more evidently laboured, are less happy; but not one is wholly destitute of points that appeal to the feelings, surprise by their unexpectedness, fascinate by their plaintive character, or charm by their ingenuity.

Frederick Chopin was born in 1810, at Zelazowa-Wola, near Warsaw, and died in Paris on the 17th of October, 1849. He was buried in the cemetery of Père la Chaise, between the tombs of Bellini and Cherubini. His obsequies were celebrated with great pomp at the Madeleine, Mozart's *Requiem* forming part of the service, in accordance with a desire which Chopin had often expressed.

LIEDER, Miss ANTOINETTE STERLING. *Schubert.*

"DIE LETZTE HOFFNUNG."

Hie und da ist an den Bäumen
  Manches bunte Blatt zu seh'n,
Und ich bleibe vor den Bäumen
  Oftmals in Gedanken steh'n.
Schaue nach dem einen Blatte,
  Hänge meine Hoffnung dran,
Spielt der Wind mit meinem Blatte,
  Zittr' ich was ich zittern kann.

Ach, und fällt das Blatt zu Boden,
  Fällt mit ihm die Hoffnung ab;
Fall' ich selber mit zu Boden,
  Wein', auf meiner Hoffnung Grab.

DER TOD UND DAS MÄDCHEN.

DAS MÄDCHEN. Vorüber, ach! vorüber,
  Geh', wilder Knochenmann!
Ich bin noch jung; geh', Lieber,
  Und rühre mich nicht an.

DER TOD. Gieb deine Hand, du schön und zart Gebild;
  Bin Freund, und komme nicht zu strafen.
Sei gutes Muths! ich bin nicht wild;
  Sollst sanft in meinen Armen schlafen.

"AUF DEM WASSER ZU SINGEN."

Mitten im Schimmer der spiegelnden Wellen,
  Gleitet, wie Schwäne, der wankende Kahn:
Ach, auf der Freude sanft schimmernden Wellen,
  Gleitet die Seele dahin, wie der Kahn.
Denn von dem Himmel herab auf die Wellen,
  Tanzet das Abendroth rund um den Kahn.

Ueber den Wipfeln des westlichen Haines,
  Winket uns freundlich, der röthliche Schein;
Unter den Zweigendes östlichen Haines,
  Säuselt der Calmus im röthlichen Schein.
Freude des Himmels und Ruhe des Haines,
  Athmet die Seel' im erröthenden Schein.

Ach, es entschwindet mit thauigem Flügel,
  Mir auf den wiegenden Wellen die Zeit.
Morgen entschwindet, mit schimmernden Flügel,
  Wieder, wie gestern und heute, die Zeit:
Bis ich auf höherem strahlenden Flügel,
  Selber entschwinde der wechselnden Zeit.

THE MESSIAH IN PARIS.*

The history of the auditions of Sacred Harmony will be like that of the Concerts Populaires. The two enterprises had the same Unknown before them; both, conducted frankly and boldly, succeeded at once. In a little time more, the process of assimilation will be complete. We shall have nothing to desire except the opportunity of applauding Beethoven, Mozart, and Weber, Handel, Bach, and Mendelssohn, elsewhere than in a circus. It is vain to disguise with flowers the features of an equestrian theatre. We shall never be able to palliate the disgrace for Paris, a place, after all, sincerely fond of music, not to possess a single grand concert hall, when London boasts of three or four. Are there not in our country intelligent capitalists? The musical festival with which the auditions of Sacred Harmony were resumed at the Cirque, had a charitable object, to which Madame la Maréchale MacMahon contributed by her presence. The House of the Providence of Sainte-Marie was destined to profit by the large returns, the prices of admission being doubled. Once more did the joyous and graceful melodies, the choruses full of grandeur and brilliancy, resound; once more did the public applaud, cry "*bis*," and acclaim both singers and conductor. *The Messiah* has decidedly entered into our manners. The profound impression of its early days here still subsists in its entirety; the work has forced itself on us, partly by its high value, and a little by right of conquest. We ought to rejoice at this magnificent result, which, fifteen months ago, never entered the dreams of the most sanguine. *The Messiah*, however, does not monopolise success. *The Passion* and *Judas Maccabæus* have already proved this, and *The Creation* will come in turn. There are two new features; the interpretation and the text. The singers to whom M. Ch. Lamoureux, last winter, entrusted the solos in Handel's score, have been replaced by others. The exigences of theatrical management will frequently impose such changes so long as oratorio music has not spread here sufficiently to have, as in England, singers who devote themselves exclusively to it. Madame Patey, who sang the contralto airs, is one of the artists of whom we are speaking. She sings only at concerts, more especially at concerts of sacred music and festivals, the best part of which is reserved for works of Handel, Mendelssohn, or Bach. With Sims Reeves, Miss Edith Wynne, and a few others, Madame Patey holds the sceptre of oratorio in London; and Thursday's audition sufficed to convince us that the great reputation she has made among her compatriots is legitimately acquired. She possesses a superb voice, of somewhat variable character in the higher register; its sonority is ample, pure, and frank in the medium and lower notes. Her style, noble and broad, Madame Patey owes as much to perfect musical feeling as to tradition, of course, permanently preserved in England. Endless bravos and recalls burst forth after " Oh, thou that tellest ! " " He was despised," " and " He shall feed His flock," which

---

* From the *Revue et Gazette Musicale*.

Madame Patey finishes most charmingly. This was enthusiasti-
cally encored. After Madame Patey, it is to Madame Brunet-
Lafleur that the largest amount of praise is due, some of the
inflexions of her charming soprano voice being exquisite in " I
know that my Redeemer liveth." The chorus and orchestra,
disciplined with the care for which M. Lamoreux is so well known,
were perfect in *ensemble* and spirit. " For unto us a child is
born" obtained the inevitabl' encore. As regards the French
text, it is no longer the barbarous translation we were compelled
to use for want of another. M. Victor Wilder's version is correct
from a linguistic point of view, and not false to musical expression,
as is too frequently the case.   CH. BANNELIER.

AN INTERVAL OF FIVE MINUTES.

SONATA, in G major, for Pianoforte and Violin.* *Mozart.*

(Second performance at the Popular Concerts.)

Adagio (Introduction)—G major; leading to
Allegro—G minor.
Andantino cantabile (with variations)—G major.

Madlle. MARIE KREBS and
Madame NORMAN-NÉRUDA.

This sonata, composed in 1781, is one of a set of six
sonatas for pianoforte and violin, composed at various periods,
but published simultaneously at Vienna, by Artaria, in 1781.
The principal themes of each movement are subjoined :—

Introduction.

---

* No. 11 of Mozart's Sonatas for Pianoforte and Violin, edited
by CHARLES HALLÉ—published by CHAPPELL and Co. 50, New
Bond Street.

Allegro (leading theme).

(Second theme.)

(Codetta.)

Finale (theme).

andante cantabile.

p Violin.

652

Variation, No. 1.

Violino *tacet.*

Variation, No. 2.

Violin. *mf*

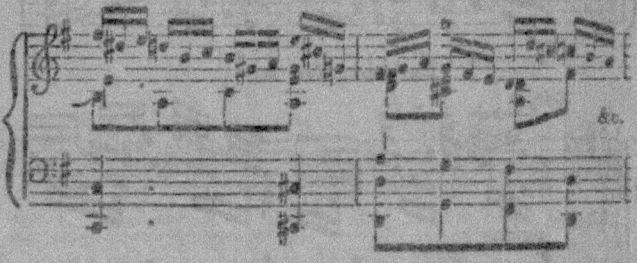

653

Allegretto—finale.

It will be observed here that the theme which was first given out as *andante cantabile* now appears as *allegretto*, without the alteration of a single note. The succeeding *coda* will speak for itself.

The Sonata in G major was first introduced by Madame Arabella Goddard and Herr Joachim, at the twenty-ninth concert of the thirteenth season—March 27, 1871.

END OF THE FIVE HUNDRED AND SECOND CONCERT.

J. MALLETT, PRINTER, 59, WARDOUR STREET, SOHO, LONDON.

SATURDAY POPULAR CONCERTS.

SATURDAY AFTERNOON, JAN. 30th, 1875.

PROGRAMME.

QUARTET, in E flat, for two Violins, Viola, and
Violoncello...*Mozart.*

Madame NORMAN-NÉRUDA,
MM. L. RIES, STRAUS, and PIATTI.

SONG, "There is a green hill far away."................*Gounod.*

Signor FEDERICI.

AIR with **VARIATIONS**, in F major, Op. 34, for
Pianoforte alone..*Beethoven.*

Dr. HANS VON BÜLOW.

SONATA, in G minor, Op. 65, for Pianoforte and Violoncello...*Chopin.*

Dr. HANS VON BÜLOW and Signor PIATTI.

SONG, " Pietà, Signore."....................................*Stradella.*

Signor FEDERICI.

QUARTET, in A major, Op. 26, for Pianoforte, Violin,
Viola, and Violoncello.......................................*Brahms.*

Dr. HANS VON BÜLOW, Madame NORMAN-NÉRUDA,
Herr STRAUS, and Signor PIATTI.

Conductor - - Sir JULIUS BENEDICT.